THE
COOKIE STALL

(🅐rt)

Written by
Jonathan Litton

Illustrated by
Magalí Mansilla

One morning, Suzy and Max were selling homemade cookies outside their house to make some extra pocket money.

They waited for customers but nobody stopped to buy their cookies. Everyone walked straight past! Why?

"The cookies look a bit plain," said Suzy.
"Maybe we could decorate them?"
"Yes!" Max replied. "We could make them
look like stars and rockets."

3

Back in the kitchen, they found colored icing and special pastry brushes. They got to work painting and decorating their cookies.

The cookies looked colorful and tasty, but
still no one stopped to buy them.

Their art teacher, Mr. Doodle, walked past.
Max called out, "Would you like a cookie, sir?"
"Yes, please," said Mr. Doodle.
"Mmmm, it's delicious!" he added.

"But I didn't realize you were selling cookies. You need to attract people's attention."

"How do we do that?" asked Suzy and Max. "Hmmm," thought Mr. Doodle. "Why don't you go and look at some stores? You'll get some ideas there. I'll look after your stall while you're gone."

"Ooh, here's a cake shop, Max," said Suzy.
"The cakes are all on cake stands and they
look so pretty and yummy!" she added.

"The fruit and veg shop is colorful, too," said Max.

"But the shoe shop looks very serious!"

"Let's make our stall bright and colorful," said Suzy.

"That way, we'll get lots of customers!"

They ran all the way back to their stall.
"Did you get lots of ideas?" Mr. Doodle asked.

"Yes!" said Suzy. "I'm going to build a
tower of plates to display the cookies."
"And I'll decorate the table," added Max.

Suzy and Max worked hard and soon their stall was transformed. "It's really bright and fun," said Suzy, "and the cookies look so tasty!"

"Now that the cookies are nicely displayed everyone will want to come and look," Max said.

A few people stopped by.
"Decorating the cookies and the stall really helped." said Max. "But is there anything else we could do?"

"We could paint a sign so that people notice our stall from across the street," suggested Suzy.

Back in the kitchen, Max and Suzy got to work. They found paint, paintbrushes, and paper, but then...

They were so excited, they bumped into each other. Blobs of paint went everywhere!

"Oh no! Our sign is ruined!" they cried.
"Let's ask Mr. Doodle what to do," said Max.
"How can we fix our sign, Mr. Doodle?"
asked Suzy.

Cookies

"Art doesn't need to be neat! Why don't you make
the splats part of the design?" he suggested.

Mr. Doodle showed them how to use colored splashes to decorate their cookie sign.

"Wow, that looks so cool!"
Max and Suzy agreed.

"How will I paint the star cookies?" asked Suzy.
"We don't have any green paint."
"And we don't have any orange paint for
the rockets either," Max added.

"You have everything you need to make orange and green right in front of you," said Mr. Doodle. "Just mix two of these colors together."

Suzy and Max mixed their paints.
"If you mix blue and yellow paint,
you get green!" said Suzy.

For sale

"And red and yellow mixed together make orange," laughed Max. "More red paint makes a darker orange, and more yellow paint makes a lighter orange."

Suzy and Max hung up their sign.
Customers flocked to their colorful stall!

BRAVO!

Yum!

woof!

The cookies sold out so fast that
soon there were only crumbs left.

"Well done!" said Mr. Doodle.
"Your design for the cookie stall and
your painted sign made all the difference!"

cookies

for sale

Let's talk
about art!

The art behind the story

Let's look at the problems Suzy and Max faced
in the story. Turn to the page numbers for help,
or find the answers on the next page.

p.4

p.14

Art everywhere

Max and Suzy created some great artwork
in the story, including colorful cookies
and a pretty sign.

*How did Max and Suzy make
the cookies more appealing?*

*How did they fix the mistake
they made on the sign?*

Your turn

Art is all around you. You can use paint on paper,
crayons on board, icing on cookies, or make sculptures
from old boxes, or collages with leaves. Have you
tried any of these? How else could you make art?

Colorful creations

Suzy and Max had red, yellow, and blue paint. These are called primary colors. When you mix primary colors, you can make new, secondary colors.

p.19

How did Max make orange paint?

Your turn

There are so many different colors and shades. What other colors can you make using the primary colors? Which two colors make purple? Why don't you experiment?

p.11

Dazzling display

Max and Suzy wanted to make their stall stand out more, so they visited the stores for ideas.

How did Max and Suzy attract customers to their cookie stall?

Your turn

Art attracts people, which is why stores use art in their displays. Look at the displays in your local stores. Which stores do you like the most? Why?

Answers

If you need help finding the answers, try reading the page again.

Art everywhere: Suzy and Max turned their cookies into stars and rockets and decorated them in bright colors. They made the paint blotches on the sign part of the design.

Colorful creations: Max made orange paint by mixing red and yellow.

Your turn: To make purple paint, you mix red and blue together.

Dazzling display: The children made their stall bright and colorful. They decorated it, displayed their cookies on a tower of plates, and painted a sign.

Quarto is the authority on a wide range of topics.

Quarto educates, entertains and enriches the lives of our readers—enthusiasts and lovers of hands-on living.

www.quartoknows.com

Author: Jonathan Litton
Illustrator: Magalí Mansilla
Consultant: Ed Walsh
Editors: Jacqueline McCann, Carly Madden, Ellie Brough
Designer: Sarah Chapman-Suire

© 2018 Quarto Publishing plc

First published in 2018 by QEB Publishing,
An imprint of The Quarto Group
6 Orchard Road, Suite 100
Lake Forest, CA 92630
T: +1 949 380 7510
F: +1 949 380 7575
www.QuartoKnows.com

A CIP record for this book is available from the Library of Congress.

ISBN 978 1 78603 283 6

9 8 7 6 5 4 3 2 1

Manufactured in Dongguan, China
TL062018

Find out more...

Here are links to websites where you will find more information on art and design.

National Gallery of Art
www.nga.gov/education/kids

Metropolitan Museum of Art
www.metmuseum.org/art/online-features/metkids/explore

FSC
www.fsc.org
MIX
Paper from responsible sources
FSC® C104723